DANITRA BROWN, CLASS CLOWN

By **Nikki Grimes**

Illustrated by **E. B. Lewis**

 HarperCollinsPublishers

 Amistad

Amistad is an imprint of HarperCollins Publishers Inc.
Danitra Brown, Class Clown
Text copyright © 2005 by Nikki Grimes
Illustrations copyright © 2005 by E. B. Lewis
Manufactured in China.
www.harperchildrens.com

Library of Congress Cataloging-in-Publication Data
Grimes, Nikki.   Danitra Brown, class clown / Nikki Grimes ;
illustrated by E.B. Lewis.—1st ed.   p. cm.   Summary: In this story told in a series
of rhyming poems, Zuri faces her fears about starting a new school year with the help
of her free-spirited best friend, Danitra.   ISBN 0-688-17290-3—ISBN 0-688-17291-1
(lib. bdg.)   [1. Schools—Fiction. 2. Best friends—Fiction. 3. Friendship—Fiction.
4. African Americans—Fiction. 5. Stories in rhyme.] I. Lewis, Earl B., ill. II. Title.
PZ8.3.G8875Dan 2005   [Fic]—dc22   2004003851

Typography by Carla Weise
1 2 3 4 5 6 7 8 9 10
❖
First Edition

To Michelle Green,
in celebration of friendship
—N.G.

To my agents,
Jeff Dwyer and Elizabeth O'Grady.
Thank you for your insight.
—E.B.L.

SCHOOL IS IN

School is in and I remember
How much I detest September:
 New classroom I have to scout
 New teacher to figure out
 New and harder math to learn
 (Numbers that make my stomach churn)
 New bullies to face or fear
 (Perhaps I should slip out of here)
But then, Danitra hops in, grinning
and all my gloomy thoughts go spinning.

"Z" IS FOR ZURI

The first day of school
is always the same.
The new teacher pauses
when she calls my name.
She asks what it means.
It's the moment I dread.
I squirm like a turtle
and tuck in my head.
I whisper the answer
and cringe when I hear
giggles rising and popping
like balloons in my ear.
Then Danitra Brown pokes me
three times in my side.
I lift up my head, and
repeat with more pride;
"My name means beautiful,
wonderful, good.
Anyone with half a brain
would steal it, if she could."

MISS VOLCHEK

Everyone loved Miss Wexler,
the teacher we had last year.
She called us Miss and Mister.
Too bad she's no longer here.

Miss Volchek's our new teacher.
She calls us by our first names.
She treats us like small children,
and nothing is quite the same.

Miss Wexler spoke in whispers.
Miss Volchek raises her voice.
She picks what books we read now.
Miss Wexler gave us a choice.

Miss Volchek gives us quizzes
with no warning in advance,
and still Danitra tells us
that we should give her a chance.

A WORLD AWAY

Miss Volchek warned us not to speak.
"Stop chattering, you two."
But keeping quiet all day was
impossible to do.
Obeying will be easier
beginning with today.
Miss Volchek made Danitra sit
three stinking rows away.

LUNCHTIME

Danitra won't swap
but is willing to share
her lunch box treats.
She doesn't care
that some kids laugh
at her corn bread square
spread with tuna,
or that people stare
at her peanut-butter sandwich
stuffed with pear.
(Her dessert of black olives
is what raises my hair!)
But that's my Danitra,
feasting on fare
nobody else
would even dare.

CLASS CLOWN

Last week, I scribbled one dumb note:
"I think Wardell is cute," I wrote.

I passed it to Danitra Brown,
but Luther snatched it, turned around

and, in a singsong voice, he read
my note. (I wished that I were dead!)

Danitra sprang up from her seat.
She twirled, and leaped, and stomped her feet.

The class laughed at Danitra's dance,
and while they laughed, I had a chance

to grab my note—which was her plan,
though I was slow to understand.

Danitra acted like a clown
for *me*. That's my Danitra Brown.

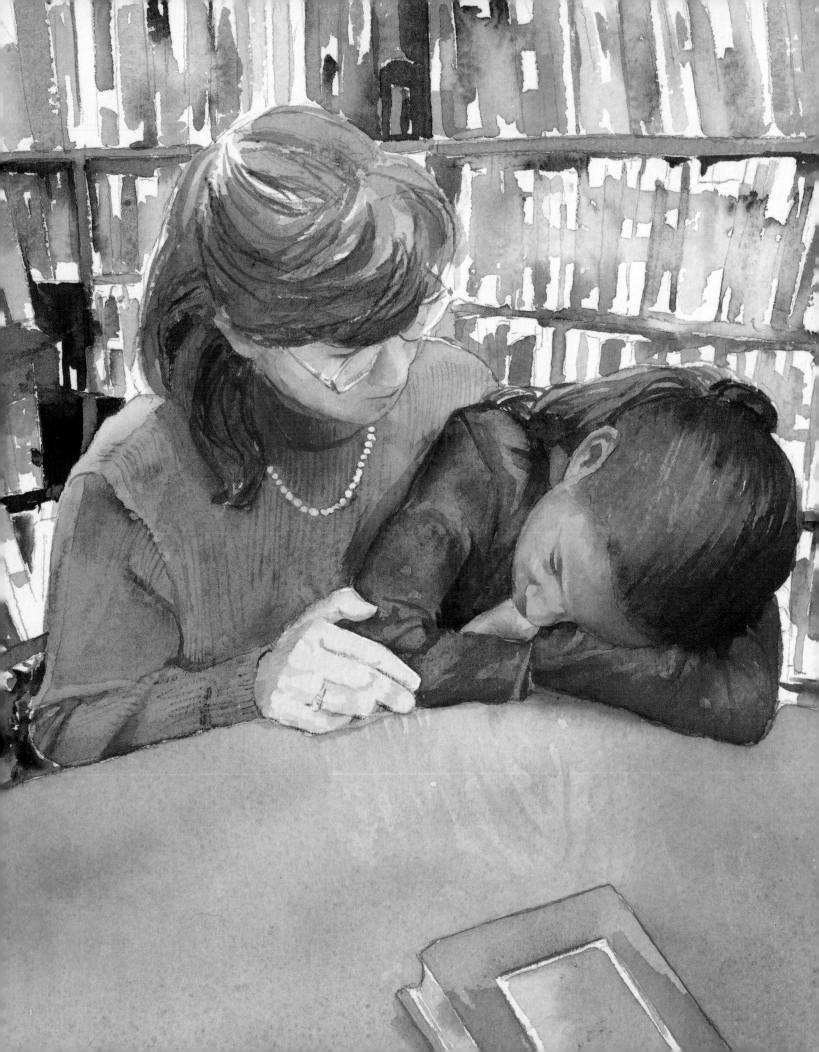

A FRIEND IN NEED

My mom was very sick last month,
I think the whole school knew.
The doctor thought that she might die
and I believed it, too.

For days, I acted unafraid.
I wouldn't even frown.
But then one day, out of the blue
I suddenly broke down.

I cried inside the library.
I hid behind a book.
I felt as if my heart would split.
From head to toe, I shook.

Danitra wasn't there that day.
I felt so all alone
until Miss Volchek pulled me close
as if I were her own.

HOMEWORK

Serious homework requires a snack.
I serve buttered popcorn before we crack
our math books open, then let out a moan.
Danitra says it's too early to groan.
But math problems make my brain cells go numb.
In no time, I'm screaming, "That's it! I'm too dumb!"
"No, you're not!" says Danitra. "So don't fill your head

with ideas like that. Get a tutor instead."
I feel mortified. She reads my mind
and whispers, "We *all* need help sometime."
I sniffle and say, "Tomorrow I'll see
if Miss Volchek has extra time for me."
Meantime, I study my math book again
and finish my homework as best I can.

HOCUS-POCUS

Danitra comes
and calls me from
the window.
I say good-bye
to an afternoon of play
and let her work
her weird magic.

Abracadabra

She says the right words,
waves her pencil,
and math solutions
burst like fireworks
lighting up my mind.

Hocus-pocus

I'm telling you,
it's true.
When Danitra is here,
my math problems disappear
     right
         before
            my eyes.

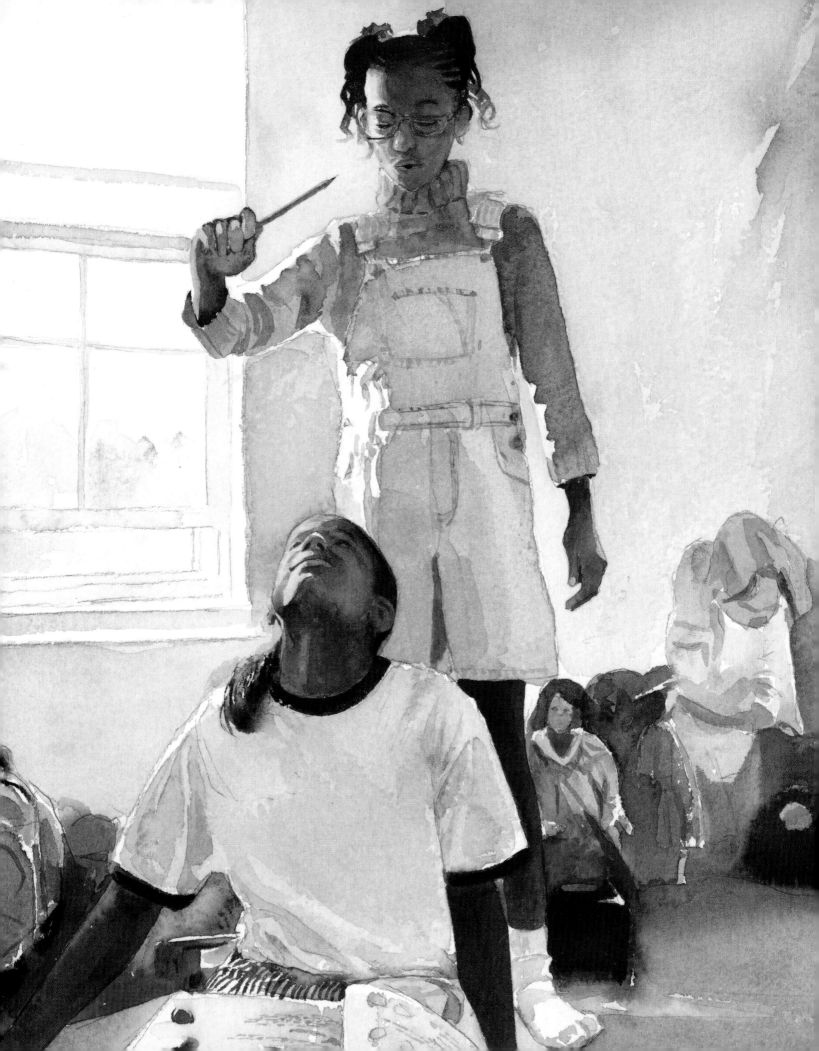

CLIMB EV'RY MOUNTAIN

I have a solo today.
The glee club
is behind me,
lips puckered
round as quarters,
*ooh-ooh*ing on cue.
I stand front and center
in an all-school assembly,
and my mouth opens,
and I'm not sure
what will come out.
A whimper? A shout?
The right chord
would be nice.
I close my eyes,
soak in the melody,
and drown any doubt.
I sing "Climb Ev'ry Mountain"
and I do.

STOMACHACHE

I have a fever.
I feel a chill.
My stomach aches.
I need a pill.
Danitra says
it's in my mind.
"You'll wake tomorrow
and you'll be fine."
I hope she's wrong.
I need my rest.
I'm way too sick
to take a test.

MATH SCORE

The math exam's been graded
and, though I did my best,
my hands are cold and sweaty.
What if I failed the test?
What if all that tutoring
didn't do the trick?
What if all my studying
didn't help a lick?

What if I get left behind?
What will I do then?
What if I retake this class
and fail all over again?
The teacher calls out, "Jackson."
I rise on wobbly knees
and sleepwalk to Miss Volchek's desk
as slowly as you please.
I take the paper from her hand.
I gulp, then check my score.
I hardly can believe my eyes—
I got an 84!

DANITRA BROWN

One of a kind hairdo
One of a kind smile
Singular appetite
Singular style
Original thinker
Ignoring every trend
Matchless tutor
Matchless friend

HALF AND HALF

The school year is half over
and half of me is glad.
That half can hardly wait till June.
The other half is sad.
My classes will be changing.
I'll move one grade ahead.
I'll sort of miss Miss Volchek.
(You tell her, and you're dead.)
I can't imagine next year will be
half as good as now,
but Danitra and I will find a way
to make it great, somehow.

Chapter I

The Sleeping Beauty

Retold by Ian Robinson
Illustrated by Gerry Embleton

DERRYDALE BOOKS

New York

A division of Crown Publishers, Inc.
New York

© Award Publications Ltd. MCMLXXX
Spring House, Spring Place
London NW5, England.

Library of Congress Catalog Number : 79-14038

All rights reserved

This edition is published by Derrydale Books, a division
of Crown Publishers, Inc., One Park Avenue
New York, New York 10016

b c d e f g h
Printed in Belgium.

Once upon a time, there lived a king and queen who were loved by all their subjects and, although they were very happy, they dearly wanted a child.

Imagine the rejoicing in the kingdom, when at last the Queen gave birth to a baby daughter. The King immediately declared a public holiday, bells rang out from every steeple in the land and everybody was invited to a christening party for the little Princess.

The guests of honour at the party were to be seven good fairies who would give the child their special blessings. To celebrate the occasion, the King ordered his jeweller to make seven beautiful gold caskets which were to be set at each of the fairy's places in the banqueting hall.

The day of the christening arrived and all the guests began to assemble in the hall.

"This is the happiest moment of my life!" the King whispered to the Queen and kissed her on the cheek.

Just as the ceremonies began, there was a noise at the back of the hall and an ugly old woman walked boldly up to the King.

"So! You were about to start without me, were you?" she cried.

At this the crowd were very surprised — the old woman was a fairy who lived all by herself far away in the wild woods. It was such a long time since anyone had seen her that the King and Queen had forgotten to invite her to the christening!

"How can I tell how sorry I am," said the King; "do come and sit with us." At this the old woman seemed happier; she sat down with the King and the banquet started.

When the meal was over, it was time for the fairies to give the Princess their blessings.

"My present is the gift of song," said the first,

"may the little Princess sing as sweetly as a nightingale on a summer's evening."

"May she be as fair as a rose and as fresh as the morning dew," added the second.

"May her eye be as sharp as a hawk's and her mind as quick as silver."

"May she ride like the wind and dance like a lamb in the springtime," said the fourth, while the fifth wished her silken hair and the laughter of a mountain brook and the sixth promised her long life and happiness.

The old woman suddenly rose to her feet and uttered a terrible curse.

"All your fine words won't save this child from my vengeance!" she hissed. "All your silly blessings have been in vain, for on the very first time she sees a spinning wheel, the Princess will prick her finger and die!"

Everybody was dismayed to hear the old woman's words. The Queen hugged her baby while the King tried to comfort her as best he could — it was of no use, the Princess was doomed to die.

But at that moment, the seventh good fairy, who had hidden herself away at the sight of the woman, stepped forward and spoke softly to the King and Queen.

"Alas, I cannot undo the evil which has been done," she said, "but I can change the spell with my own blessing for the Princess. She will *not* die when she pricks her finger, but will fall asleep for a hundred years, only to be woken by a prince from distant lands."

Although the King was overjoyed that his daughter was spared from death, he set out to make sure that no part of the bad fairy's curse should ever come true. A proclamation was read in every village; every spinning wheel in the kingdom was to be destroyed. All over the land they were piled high in the market squares and armed soldiers were told to make sure that every last one was burned to a cinder.

The years passed and the little Princess grew up to be a beautiful young girl, just as the good fairies foretold. The King and Queen were delighted to see her playing happily in the castle gardens and to hear her sweet singing drift through the cloisters. Surely no harm could ever befall

such a charming and delightful young creature?

One day, when she was exploring the castle cellars, the Princess came to a little door she had never seen before. She pushed it open, and finding a staircase on the other side, decided to climb it to see where it could lead.

As she reached the top of the stairs, the Princess saw one of the oddest sights she had ever seen. There, surrounded by coloured wools, sat an old lady spinning.

"Hello, my dear, come in," said the old lady when she saw the Princess, "come here and sit beside me." The Princess was fascinated by the spinning wheel at which the old woman sat.

"Whatever are you doing?" she asked.

"Why, spinning, of course," the old lady replied. "When I was a girl everyone could do it; now this must be the only spinning wheel left in the whole kingdom."

"Oh, do let me try!" pleaded the Princess, "it looks such fun, I'm sure you could show me what to do."

"Of course," replied the old lady and she sat the Princess down at the wheel where she started to spin. No sooner had she begun to take up the wool from the spindle, however, than she pricked her finger and fell to the ground in a deep, deep sleep.

At this the old woman let out a horrible peal of laughter.

"That will teach them to think they can outwit me!" she cried. The old woman was none other than the bad fairy in disguise — she had got her revenge at last!

When he heard the terrible news, the King was very upset. Sadly, he carried his daughter to the Royal Chambers and laid her to rest. All through the night he sat by her side in the cold, dark room, tears trickling down his cheeks.

At last, news of the terrible fate which had befallen the Princess reached the good fairy who had saved her life at her christening. She hurried to the castle at once to see the King and Queen.

"How unlucky it is that you should live to see this day," she said, "I cannot see you parted from your daughter so cruelly; if she is to sleep for a hundred years, then you and the court must do the same." As she spoke, the good fairy blew magic dust into their eyes, and the King and Queen felt themselves growing weary. Soon they fell asleep exactly as they were, sitting in front of the Princess's bed.

When the King and Queen were soundly asleep, the fairy flew from room to room scattering her magic dust wherever she went. Maids, grooms, soldiers and serving boys fell asleep where they stood and silence fell over the castle.

In the great hall the jester had just started to tell a joke when the fairy's spell sent him to sleep. The musicians fell into a deep slumber still holding their instruments, and the chancellor and the magician, who were playing a game of chess, began to snore loudly as if both were tired of waiting for the other to finish his turn. Out in the courtyard the stable lads fell asleep as they were sweeping and even the horses dozed in their stalls.

At last, when everyone in the whole castle was soundly asleep, the good fairy cast a final spell.

"You will all sleep safely for a hundred years until the Princess wakens from her slumbers." she whispered and then she made a mighty forest of briars grow up around the whole castle, all but hiding it from view, so that only the topmost towers could be seen.

So the castle remained for a hundred years. People came and went past the enchanted wood which surrounded its mighty walls and strange stories about the fate which had befallen it spread far and wide. The woods were said by some to be haunted, and people soon started to hurry past the castle as fast as their legs could carry them.

Word of the mysterious castle reached a handsome young prince from a far-away land across the sea, who was determined to see it for himself and to take the beautiful princess, mentioned in the story, for his bride.

After many days journeying, the Prince came to the tangled wood of brambles and briars.

"I am not afraid of old stories!" he told himself and started to hack aside the thorny bushes with his sword. To his astonishment, suddenly a pathway opened in the woods before him. As if by magic he found himself being led deeper and deeper through the forest, until he found himself standing before the castle walls.

Once inside the castle gate the Prince gave out a cry of amazement, for there before him, looking as though they had fallen asleep that very afternoon, lay the servants of the castle. Tools lay scattered around them; there sat a man peeling apples, there a maid with a broom sleeping on the stairs.

"This must indeed be some strange and marvellous magic!" exclaimed the Prince, rubbing his eyes in disbelief. He took up a candle-stick from the table and began to climb the stairs to the Royal apartments. As he entered the Royal Chamber, his heart gave a wild leap for before him, exactly as the old story had foretold, lay the most beautiful girl he had ever seen — the sleeping Princess.

Slowly the Prince drew nearer the bed where the sleeping beauty lay. Bending gently over her silent form, he kissed her lightly on the lips. Suddenly her eyelids fluttered and the Princess began to stretch. After all those years, the good fairy's final wish had come true. The Princess awoke and saw standing before her the handsome young Prince who had broken the spell and set her free. They fell in love at once and the Prince vowed to make her his bride.

As soon as the spell was broken, people began to wake up all over the palace. The King and Queen guessed at once what had happened and immediately gave the young couple their blessing. The sound of music and laughter came from the great hall, whilst the jester finished telling his joke.

"Your move!" cried the chancellor to the magician, and then they were dancing and singing and making merry. The forest around the castle vanished, the flags of the kingdom flew proud and clear in the breeze and messengers rode out from the palace to tell everybody what had happened.

When the wonderful news spread across the land, people came from every corner of the kingdom to welcome back the wise old King and to celebrate the marriage of the Prince and Princess. The King and Queen wept with joy to see their daughter once again so happy and everyone said what a fine pair the young couple made.

After the wedding the Prince and his bride set sail for his castle across the sea. When they arrived, everybody was charmed and delighted with the beautiful Princess and they both lived happily ever after.